SAGITTAS
ROYO

SAGITTAS
ROYO

SAGITTA: ARROW.

SYMBOL OF THOUGHT AND ACTION. ENERGY THAT PROJECTS ITSELF BEYOND THE PRESENT.

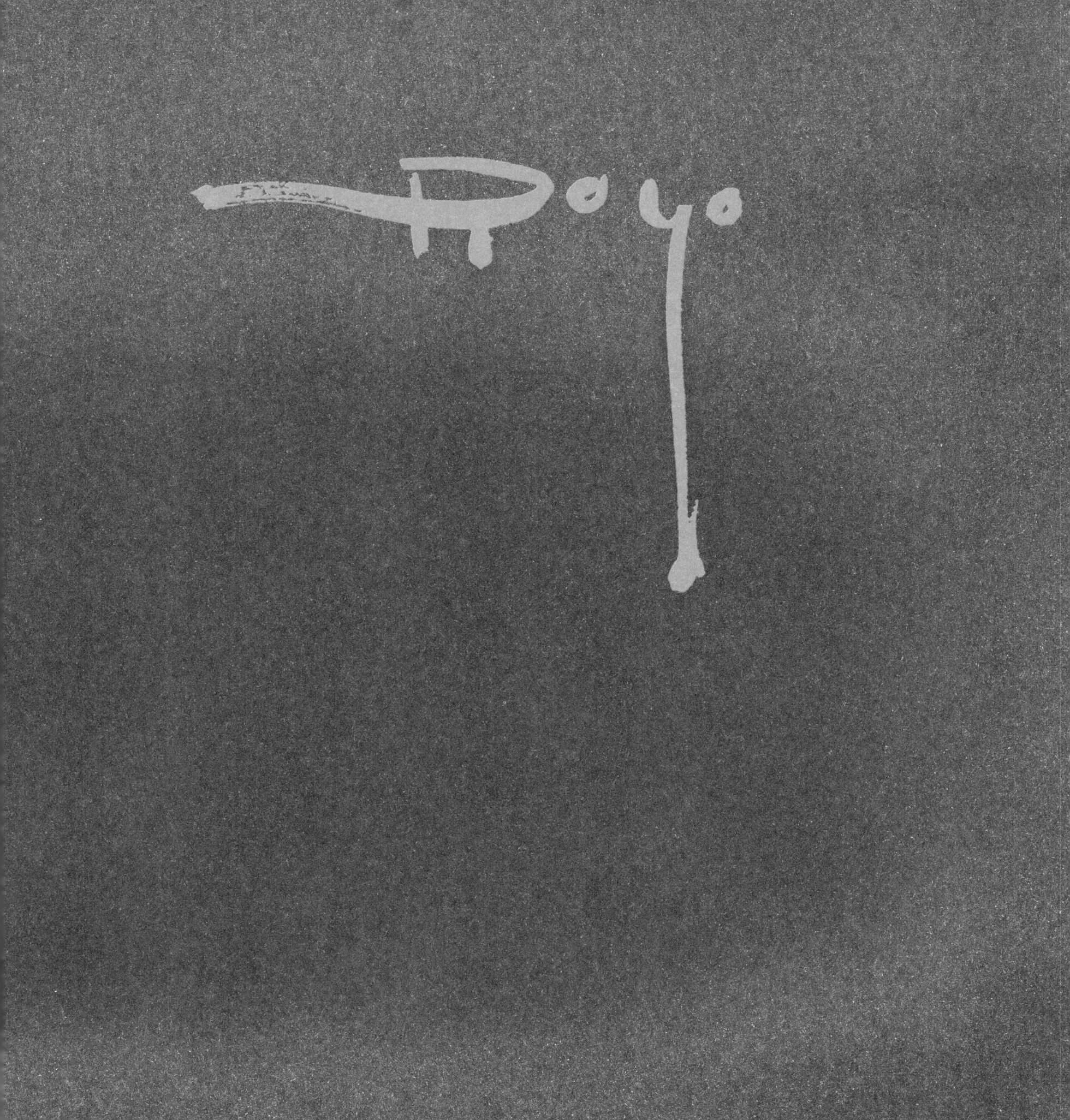

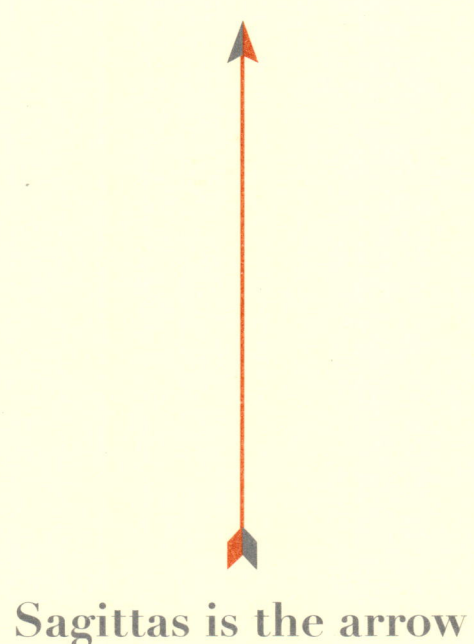

Sagittas is the arrow

Royo has chosen this classical name "Sagittas" for this exhibition, bringing together various works which revolve around the theme represented by this Latin word.

"Sagittas" is the arrow; "Sagittario" the archer. Royo's paintings portray to the open gaze of the spectator those youths crowned with flowers and ribbons shining in their nubile beauty, their arrows lancing into the air, destined to sketch an infinite bow on the horizon.

We live and walk on a bow

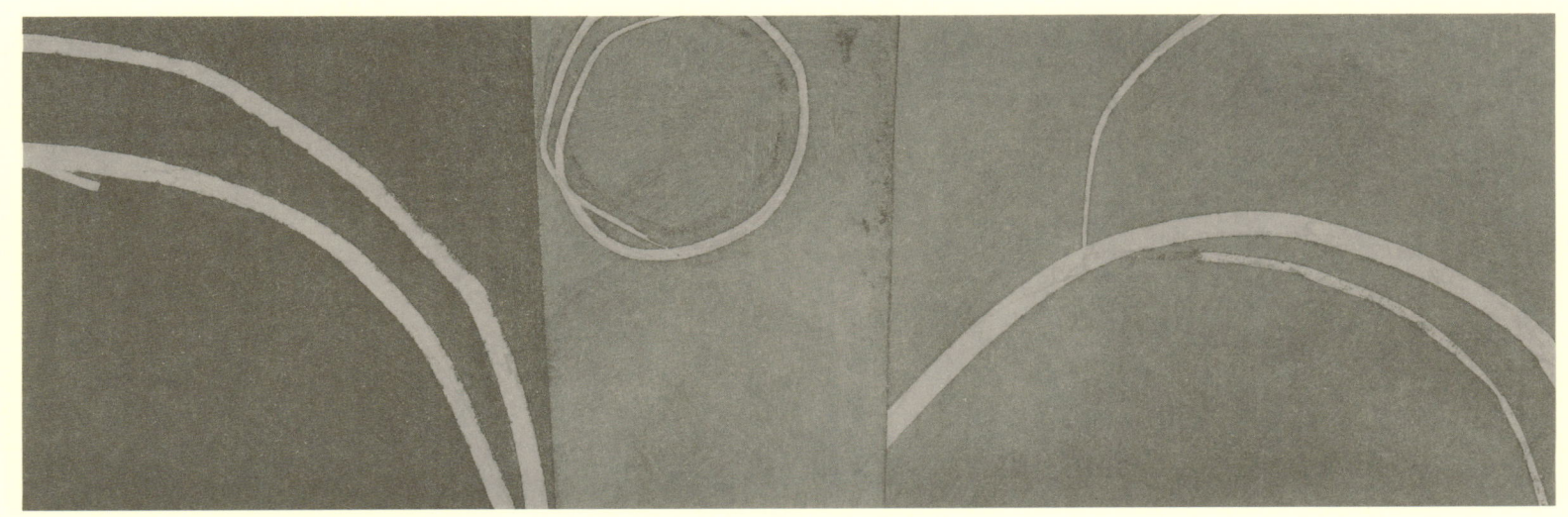

Mankind forms the centre of gravity in classical culture, we live and walk on a bow, our own steps follow the pace and sketch of an arrow in flight. A bow is the earth's curve concealing the path of the planets around the sun, a bow sketches the flight of birds. When the graceful archer, from the provoking splendour of his flesh, shoots his powerful bow, the flight curve sketched by the arrows is the same as that of the universe.

They are the dreams of ancient myths

A secret

relation beats between the painting of Royo, which elevates in category to a work of art the agile bodily movements of the archer and the silent music awakened by the arrow in nature, between the work of the artist and the curve of our own imagination; between this arrow escaping from the hands of the archer and at the same time penetrating the target heart, in the air for he who runs and the eternal beyond of the gods. They are the dreams of ancient myths, tales of the Iliad, of bucolic Virgilian, the eternal emotions of art.

Royo has chosen a geometrical formula as a symbol

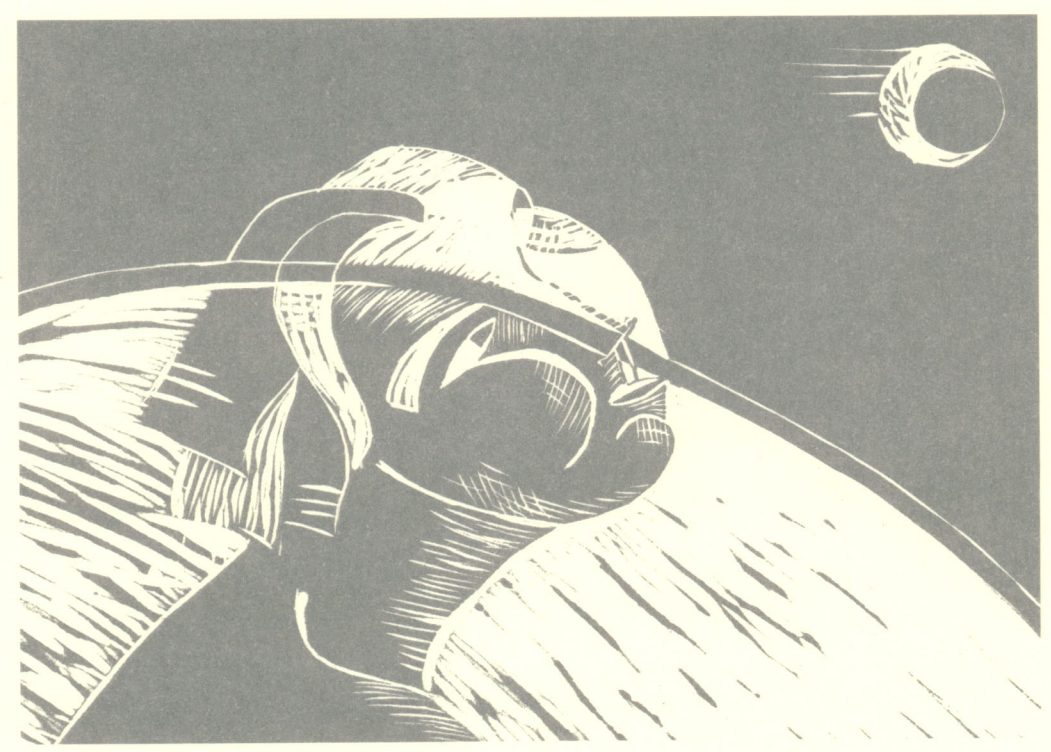

Royo has chosen a geometrical formula as a symbol. Mathematics have always been close, and geometry has always been hand in hand with art. In all pictorial creation there's an architectural depth. At the base of the architectural creations is a wide range of drawings and colours. Royo's paintings created with complete freedom of the brush on the canvas, at the same time respond to an inexhaustible spontaneity and to a geometrical discipline of classical thoughts. And from this radiates a tremendous force which comunicates with our sensitivity.

The true ecstasy of the beauty of movement

A communion exists which contrives levels of subconscious between the artist and the work of art, no different from that between the painting and the contemplator. An archer painted by Royo can conjure up the memory of an Arcady, no less alive, although a dream, it can also suppose the true ecstasy of the beauty of movement.

The aesthetic flight of the arrow never arriving at its destiny

A spirit

is never still when the archer tenses his muscles, without upsetting the ancient calm of the old works of art of the Grecoroman sculptors. In choosing the eternal theme of the bow for his painting story, and identifying this with the sketch of the arrows, Royo has given unique beauty to the dynamic movement of ecstasy; the aesthetic flight of the arrow never arriving at its destiny, the swift Achilles who never reaches the turtle, the controversy between the being who never changes and the continually changing river.

All this is the imagination

All this is the imagination of he who falls in love with a work of art. The painting is sufficient because it's language is simple and it's message direct. Only the contemplator can discover the personal interpretation.

Alberto de la Hera
Catedrático de la Universidad Complutense de Madrid
Ex-Director General de Teatro y Espectáculos

Royo ha elegido el nombre clásico *Sagittas* para una exposición que recoge diversas obras que giran en torno al tema que la palabra latina representa.

Sagittas es la flecha; Sagitario es el arquero. Los cuadros de Royo muestran a la mirada del espectador aquellos jóvenes que, coronados de flores y cintas, brillaban en el esplendor de su belleza núbil mientras lanzaban al aire las flechas destinadas a trazar un arco sobre el dibujo sin fin del horizonte.

Los hombres —y el hombre constituía el centro de gravedad de la cultura clásica— vivimos sobre un arco, caminamos sobre un arco, nuestro propio paso sigue el ritmo y el trazado de una flecha en el aire. Un arco es la curvatura de la tierra, un arco esconde el itinerario de los planetas en torno al sol, un arco traza el vuelo de las aves. Cuando el grácil arquero, desde el sugerente esplendor de su carne, dispara su poderoso arco, la curva que su flecha dibuja es la misma en la que se contiene el universo.

Late una relación secreta entre la pintura de Royo —que eleva a la categoría de obra de arte el ágil movimiento del cuerpo del arquero— y la música inaudible que la flecha despierta en la naturaleza; entre la obra del artista y la curva que nuestros ojos imaginan; entre esa flecha que escapa de las manos de quien la lanza y penetra, a la vez, en el corazón al que apunta, en el aire por el que corre y en la morada eterna de los dioses. Son sueños de la antigua mitología, de los relatos de la Ilíada, de la bucólica virgiliana, del sentimiento eterno del arte.

Royo ha elegido un símbolo que es una fórmula geométrica. Siempre estuvieron cerca las matemáticas y el arte, siempre se dieron la mano el arte y la geometría. Hay una honda arquitectura en toda creación pictórica; hay una profunda gama de dibujos y colores en el fondo de toda creación arquitectónica. Los cuadros de Royo, constituidos sobre la libertad con que se mueve el pincel sobre el lienzo, responden a la vez a una inagotable capacidad improvisadora y al rigor geométrico del pensamiento clásico. Y en ello radica la tremenda fuerza con que se comunican con nuestra sensibilidad.

Existe una comunión, que discurre a niveles de subsconsciencia, entre el artista y la obra de arte, no menor que la existente entre la obra de arte y quien la contempla. Un arquero de Royo puede suponer el recuerdo de una arcadia no por soñada menos viva; puede suponer también la realidad del éxtasis ante la belleza en movimiento. Cuando se tensan los músculos del arquero, no le es dado al espíritu permanecer inmóvil. Al elegir, para un arco completo de su historia de pintor el tema eterno del arco que se identifica con el trayecto de las flechas, Royo ha dotado de impar belleza a un movimiento dinámico del éxtasis; la estética de la flecha que nunca llega a su destino, la del veloz Aquiles que nunca alcanza a la tortuga, la de la polémica entre el ser que nunca cambia y el río que nunca es el mismo.

Todo lo cual son imaginaciones de quien se enamora de una obra de arte. Al cuadro le sobran todos los comentarios porque su lenguaje es sencillo y su mensaje es inmediato. Sólo el espectador puede conocer lo que la pintura personalmente le dice.

Alberto de la Hera

24

SAGITTAS

Sagittas towards the clouds, the horizon and beyond; Sagittas.

Sagittas

79" x 79"
Oil on canvas

Sagittas

Detail

His movements are a dance, perfection and beauty.

Sagittarius

79" x 79"
Oil on canvas

Sagittarius

Detail

The silk ribbon indicates the speed and direction of the wind.
It is the moment and the place.

El momento

79" x 79"
Oil on canvas

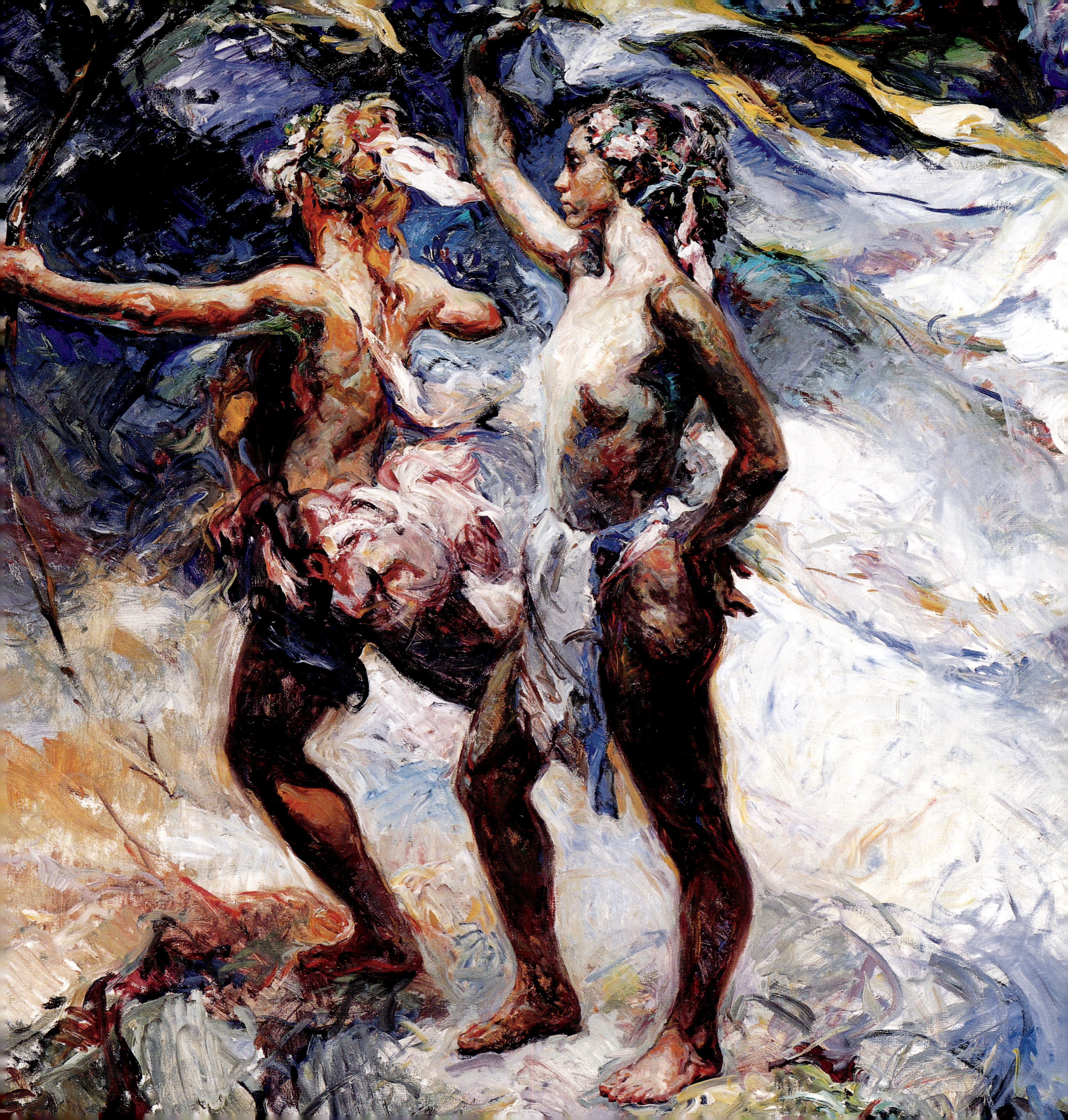

El momento

Detail

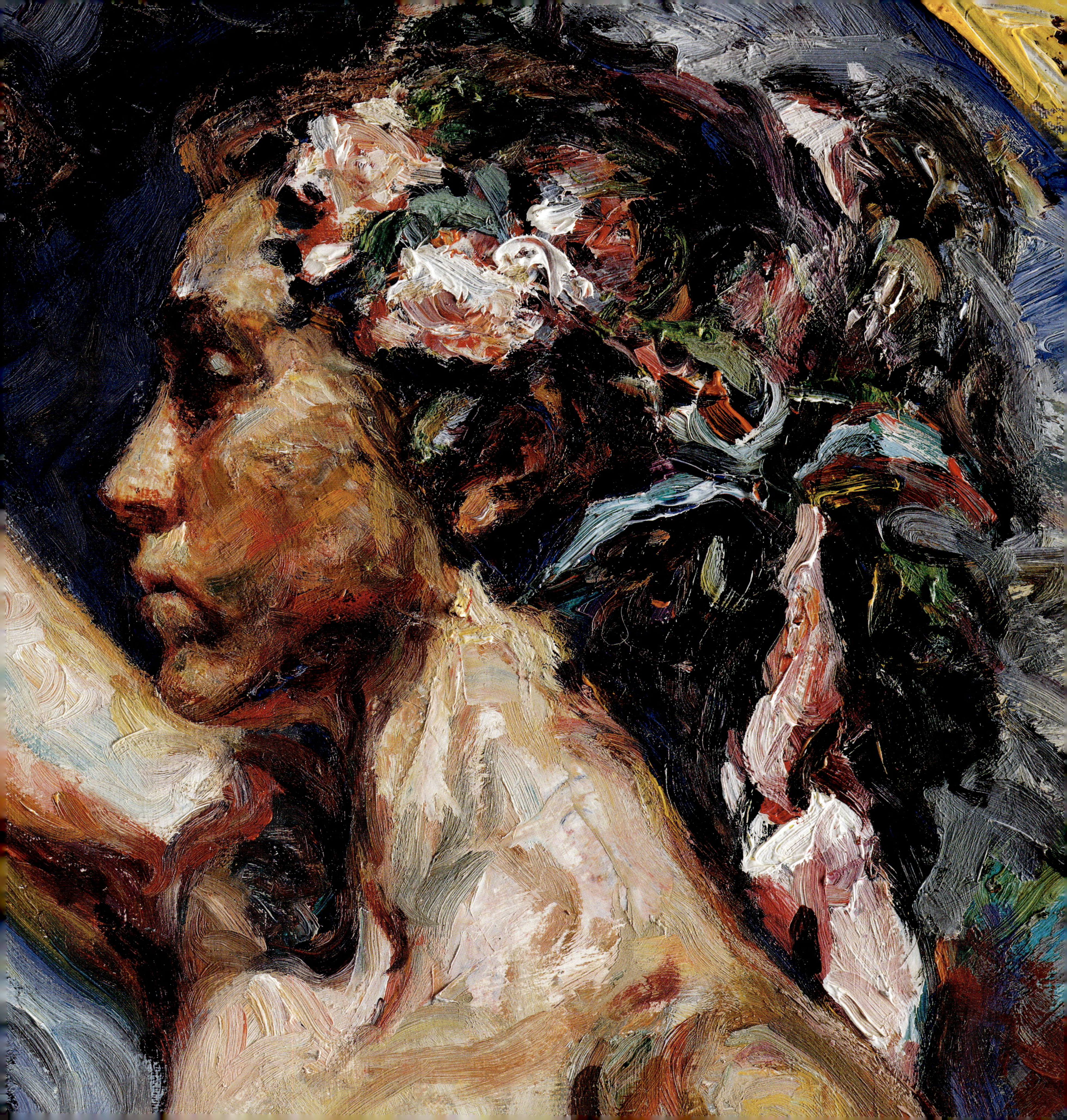

To be for a moment light.

Summussagittas

79" x 79"
Oil on canvas

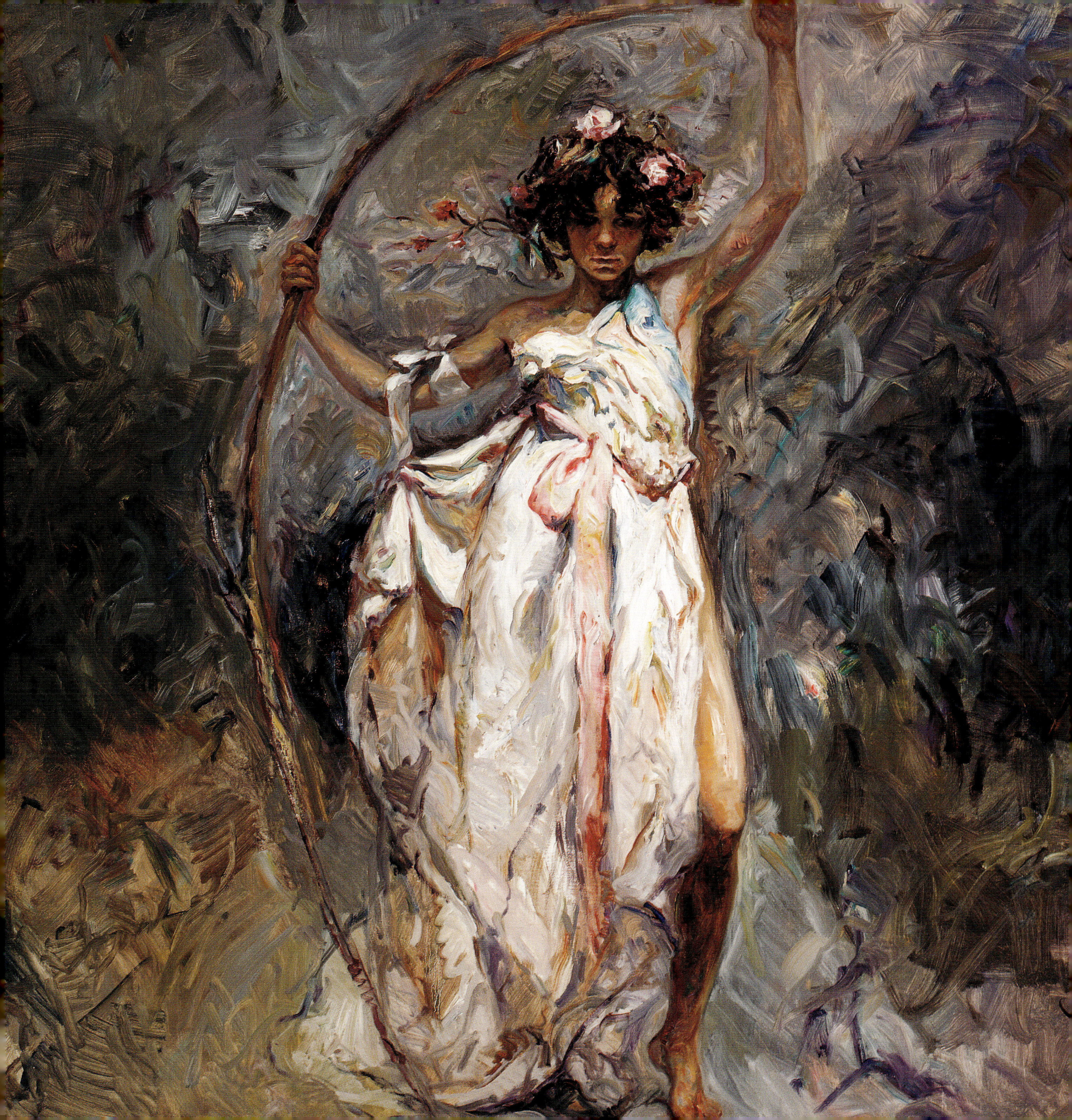

Summussagittas

Detail

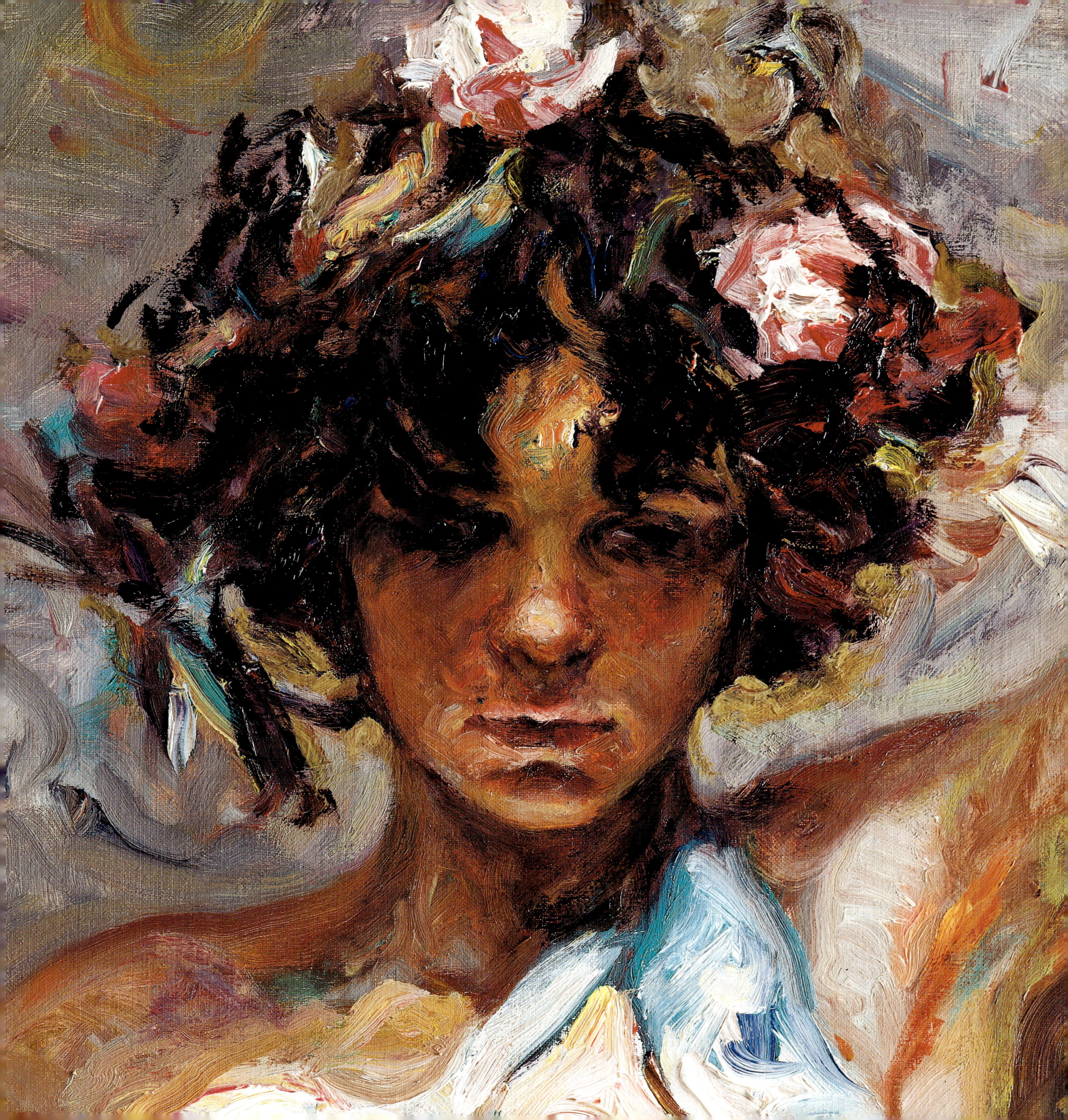

Like a weather vane from its calm, turning.

Ritmo

71" x 40"
Oil on canvas

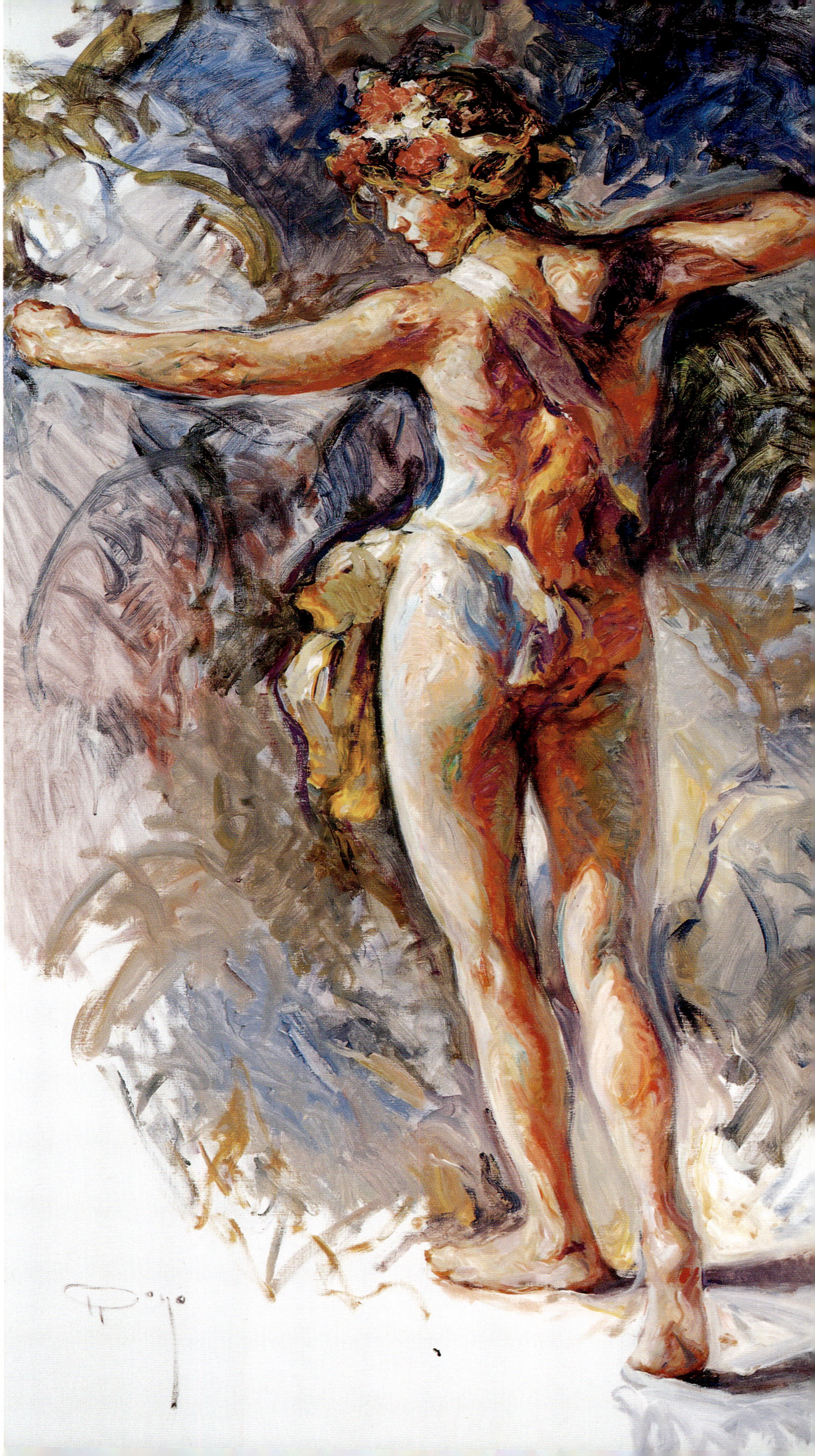

The bow's tension continues in his mind.

La espera

71" x 40"
Oil on canvas

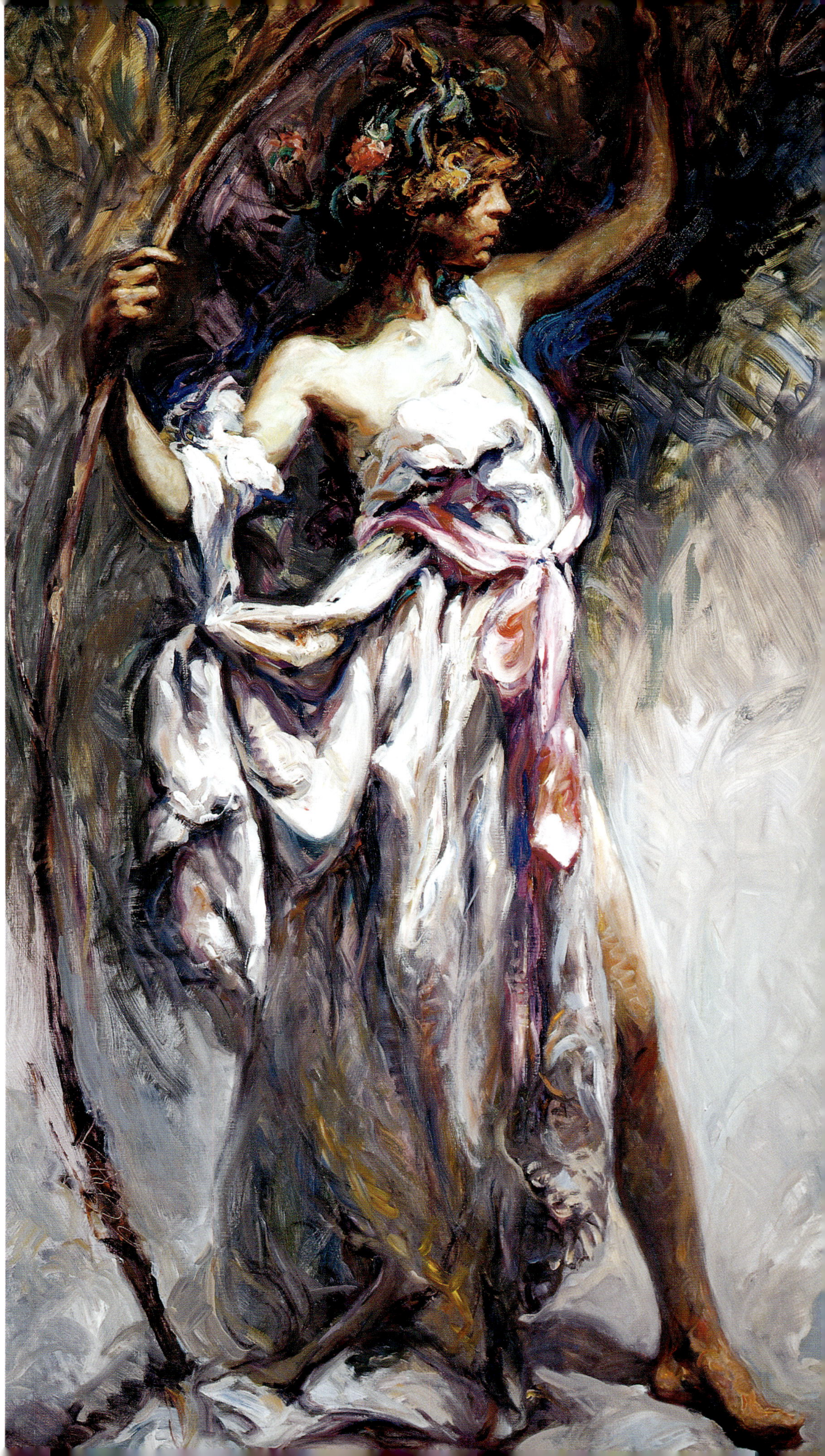

When darkness falls like your shawl the sky fills with a cover of brilliant diamonds. Dawn.

"Prima Luce"
Dawn

71" x 40"
Oil on canvas

Serigraph

IMAGE SIZE: 24-3/4" high x 45" wide
SHEET SIZE: 29-1/4" x 49 on the Paper, White Museum Board Edition
25" x 45-1/4" on PANEL, *Claybord*-TM Edition
EDITION: 250, plus proofs, PAPER, printed on White Museum Board Edition
95, plus proofs, PANEL, printed on *Claybord*-TM Edition

Prima Luce

Floral architecture, expecting in time to become stone.

Arco de triunfo

40" x 40"
Oil on canvas

49

The line is invisible but distinct.

Hastatus

40" x 40"
Oil on canvas

HASTATUS

Moving target (in the firmament).

Sagitta Lunaris

40" x 40"
Oil on canvas

53

Sagitta Lunaris

Detail

"HASTATUS"

A miracle of the sea, born from the surf.

Joven Afrodita

18" x 11"
Oil on canvas

61

Your expression is a sacred language.

La otra orilla

24" x 15"
Oil on canvas

63

Out of time, a myth.

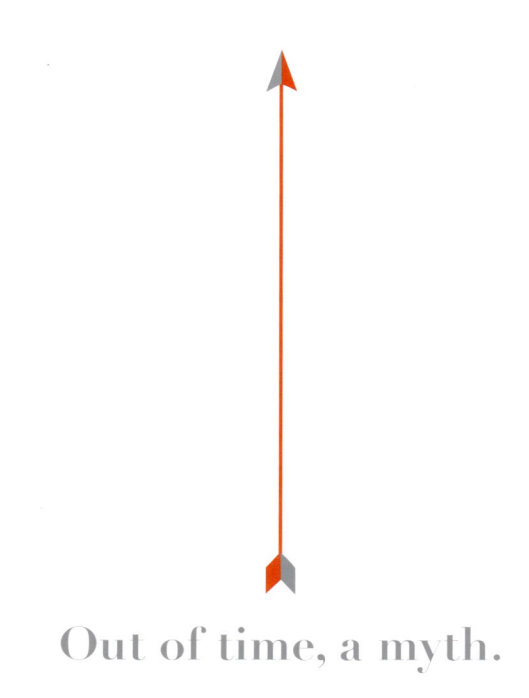

Regina Sagittas

24" x 16"
Oil on board

"Sagita"

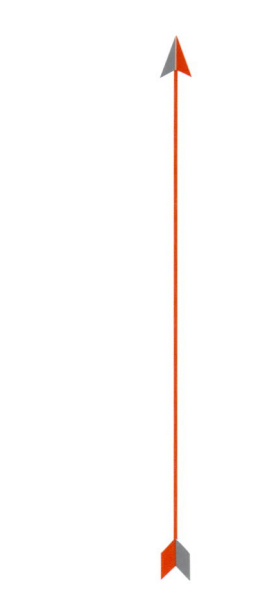

To be, in order to be a legend.

La edad de plata

24" x 16"
Oil on board

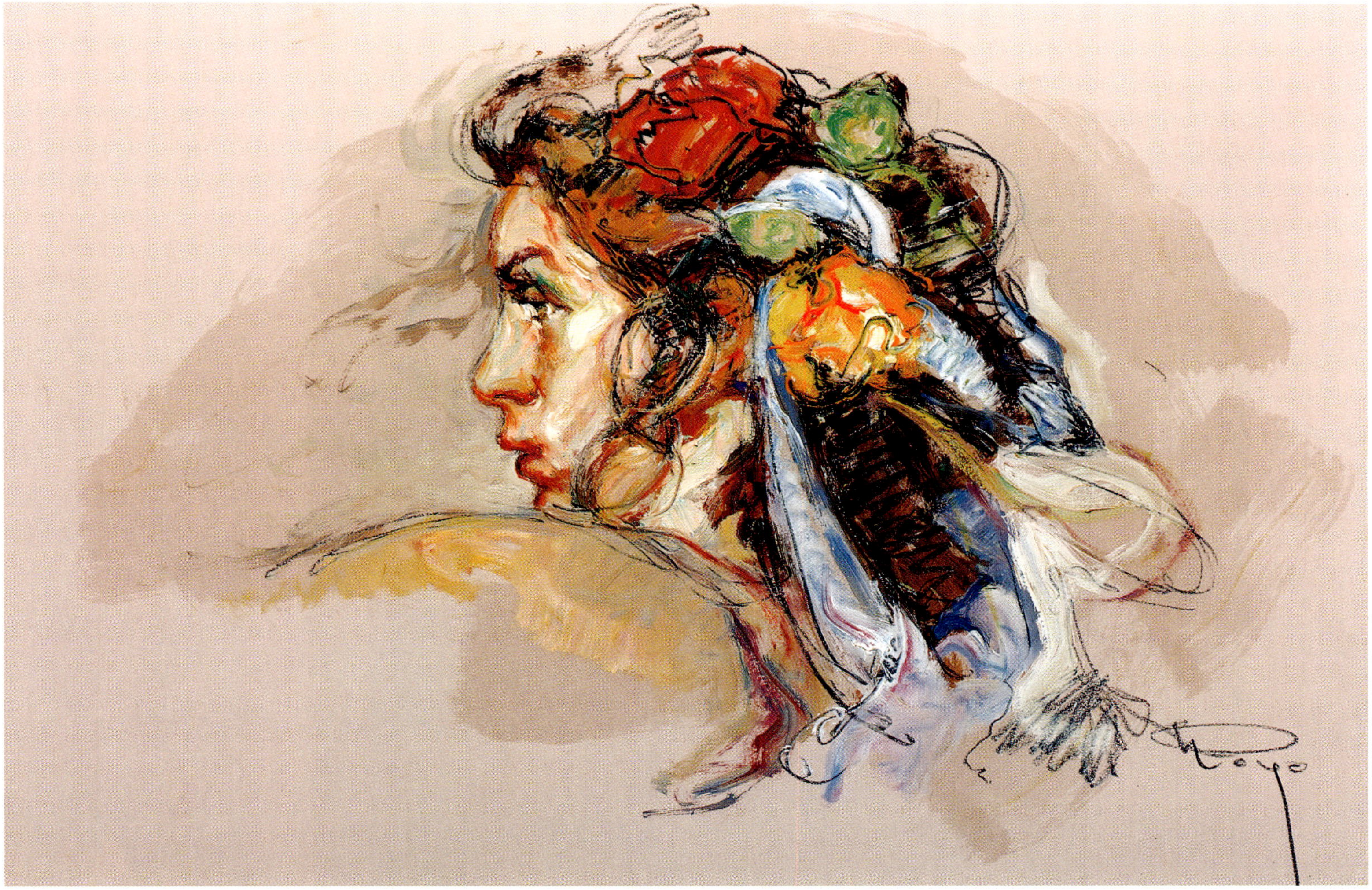

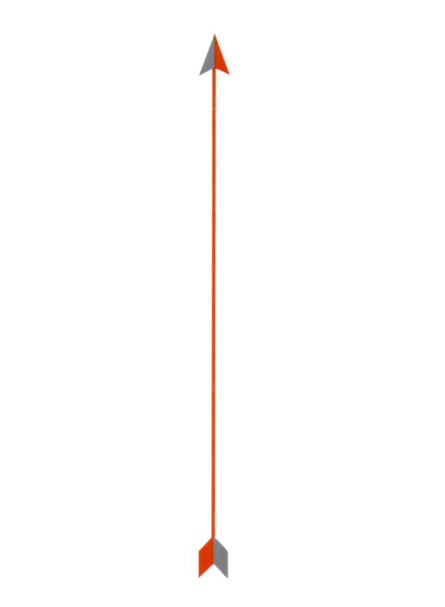

The gods are near.

Extasis

24" x 16"
Oil on board

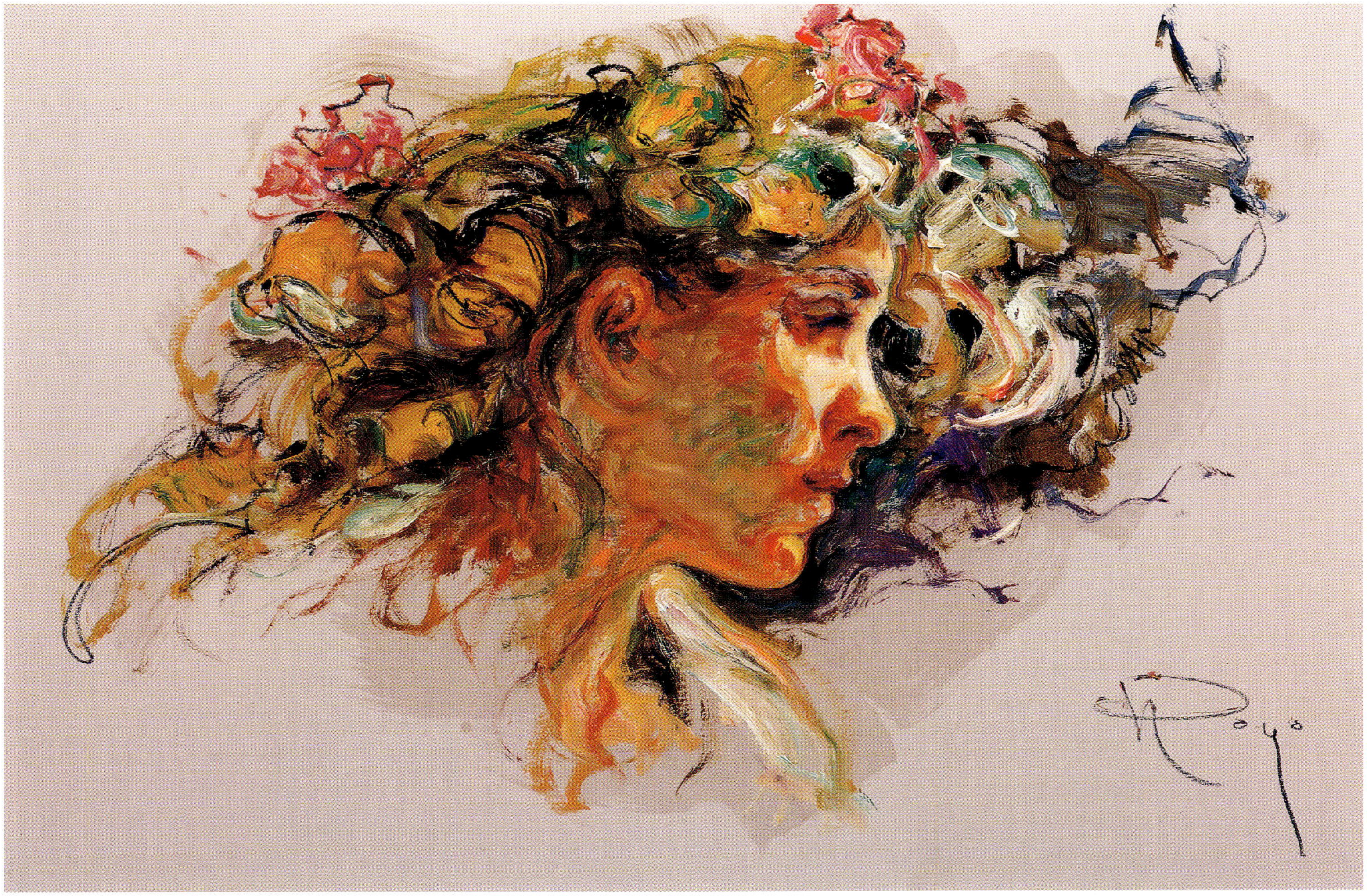
Royo

Alegoría

44" x 32"
Oil on board

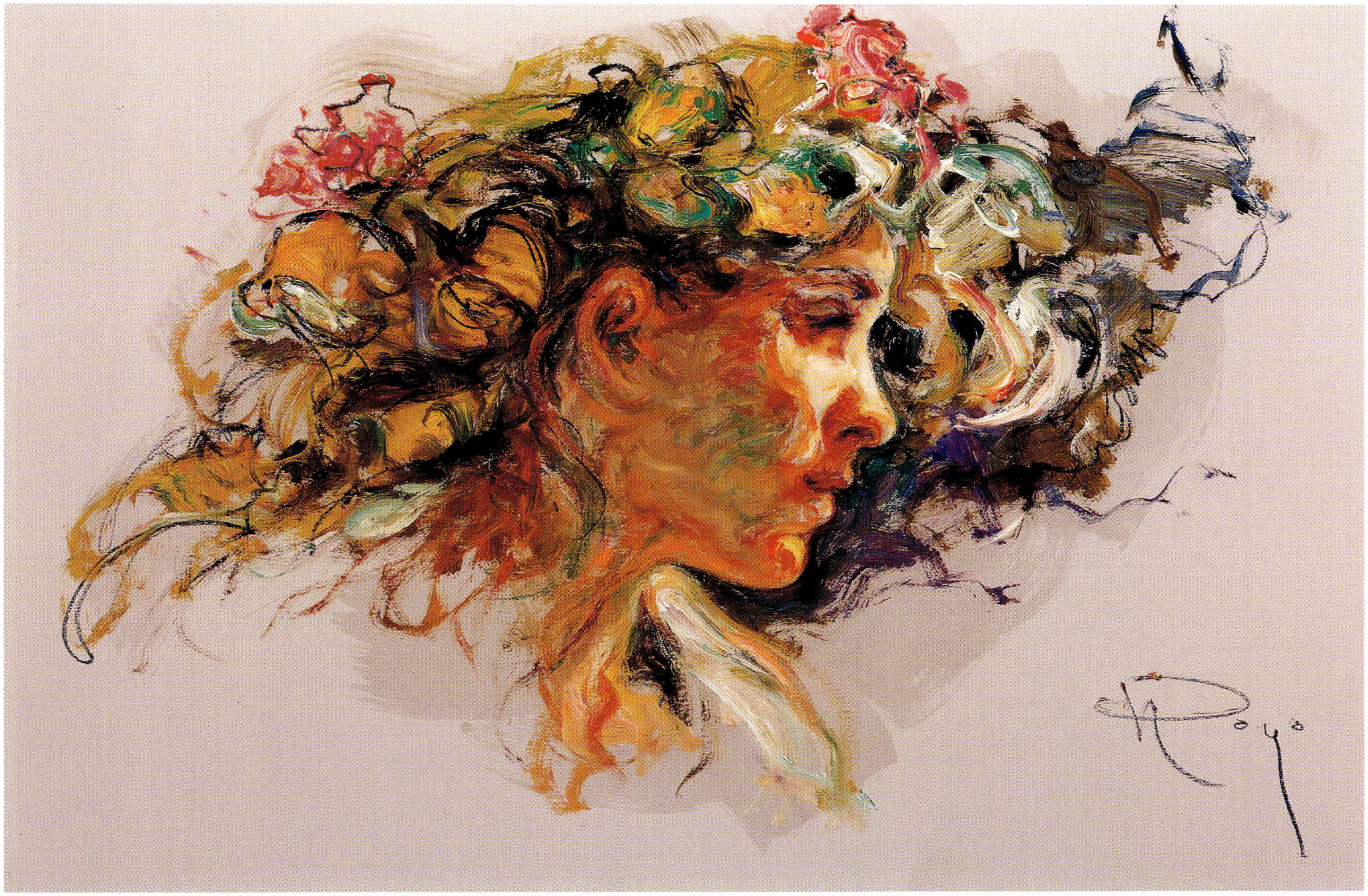

Alegoría

44" x 32"
Oil on board

70

Éter

44" x 32"
Oil on board

Study (Sagitta Lunaris)

44" x 32"
Oil on board

Study (El momento)

44" x 32"
Oil on board

Flexus

44" x 32"
Oil on board

Custos I

44" x 32"
Oil on board

Custos II

44" x 32"
Oil on board

Corpus

44" x 32"
Oil on board

SCULPTURES

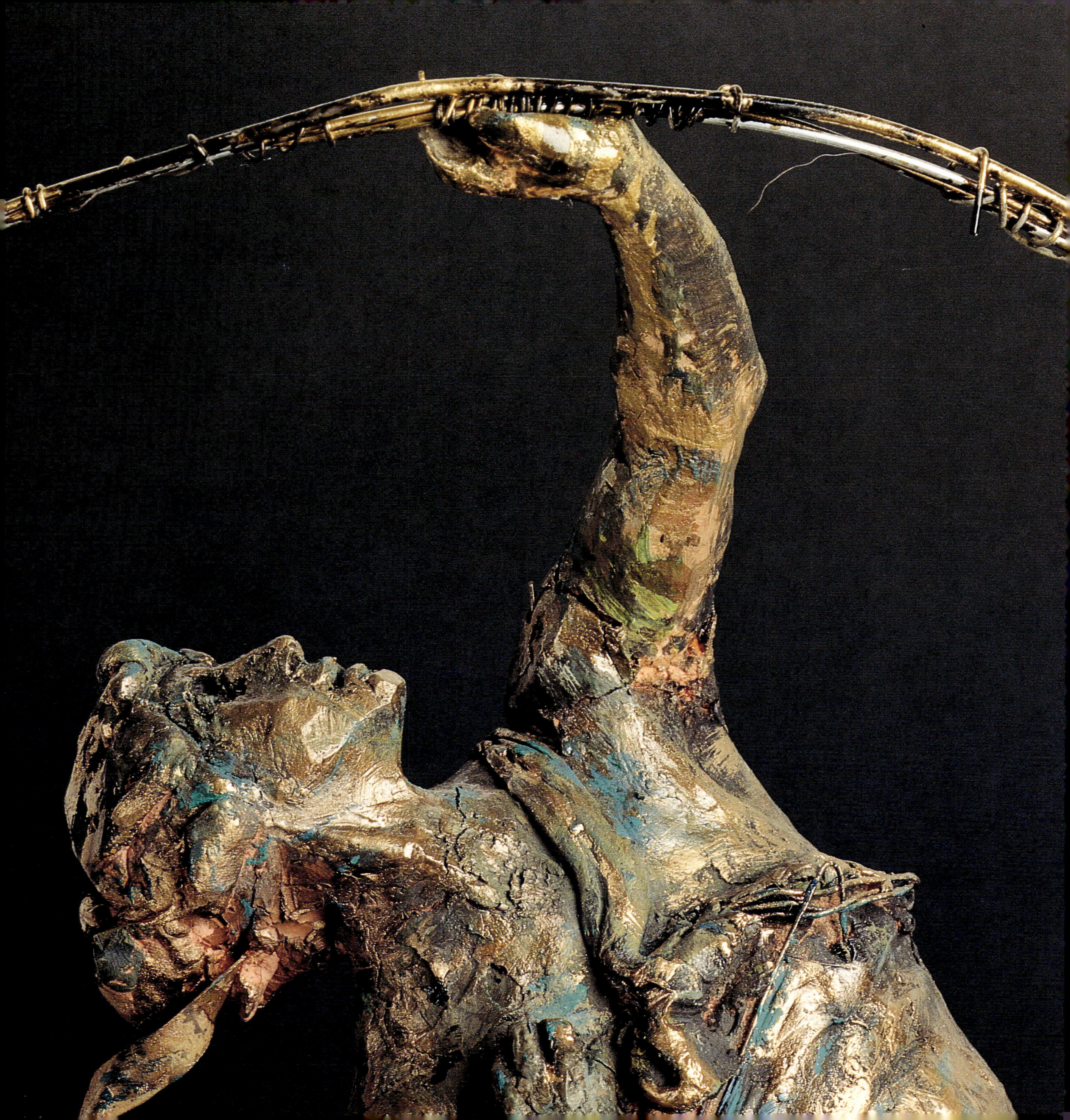

Sagitta

Detail

Sagitta

Measurements: 16" x 16"
Bronze sculpture.
Process: Lost wax.
Patina: Acid colouring torch technique.
Edition: 49 pieces.

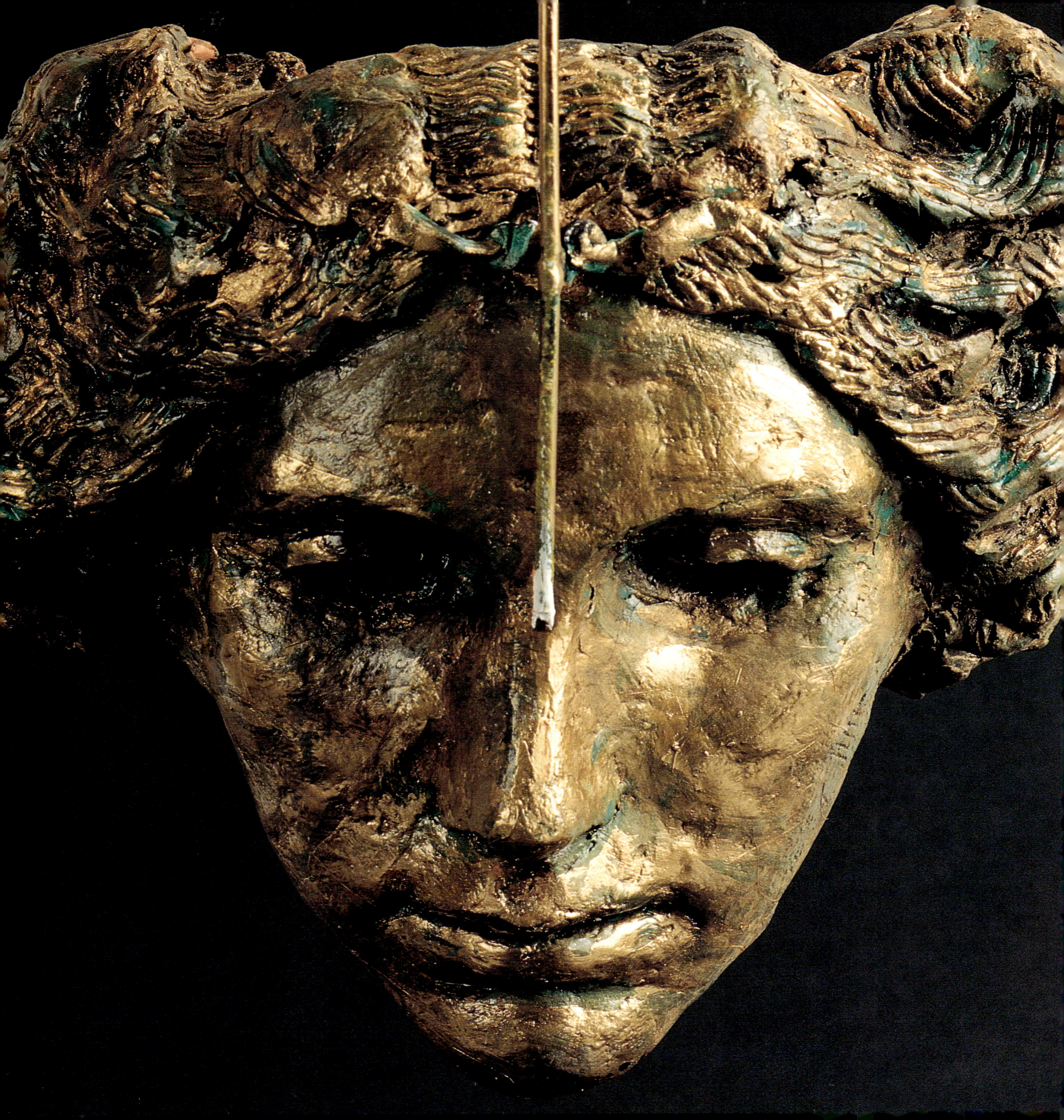

Persona

Measurements: 16" x 11"
Bronze sculpture.
Process: Lost wax.
Patina: Acid colouring torch technique.
Edition: 49 pieces.

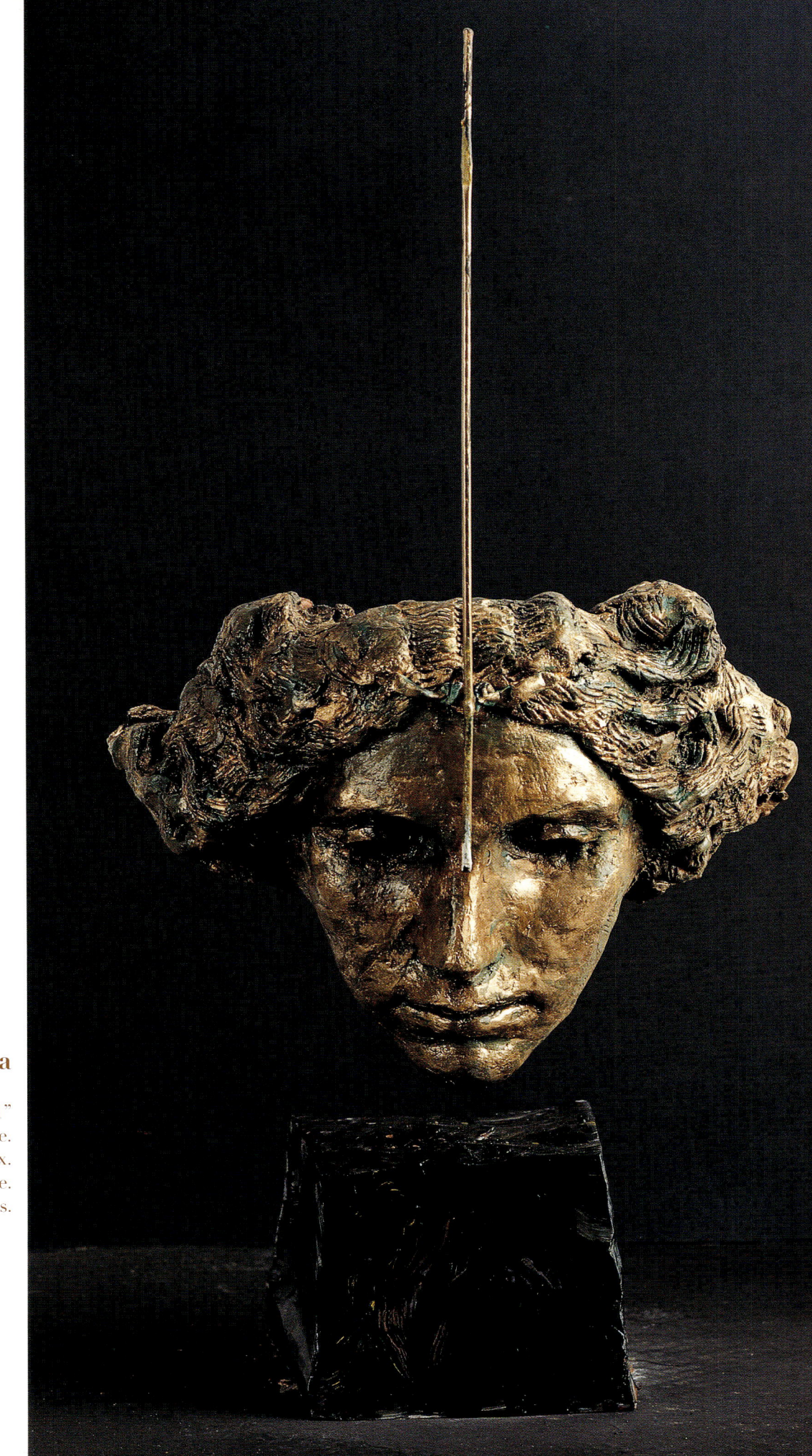

Persona

Detail

GOD IN THE PROCESS

Flowered hair crowns her. Eyes modestly averted, she raises the flowing garment draped around her, and almost seems to be dipping into a graceful bow. She is the narrator. Her motion is Shakespearean, and in a structure typical of the Elizabethan Bard, the door through which she will lead opens upon a pastoral tale of epic magnitude, winding as it does through once and future ages.

But there is a ticket to be bought before entering into the landscape of the artist's imagination. The language of Sweet William's time lacked a vocabulary complete enough to describe the incumbent drama. Coining new words proved necessary for the expression of the motivational motion of a vision that was his alone.

So too, undertaking the journey through *Sagittas*, Royo's new cycle of image poetry, requires the traveler to expand his atlas past the edges of its pages. Fortunately, unlike ancient world charts, there is no warning that

Royo says, "the painting is sufficient because its language is simple and its message direct."

"beyond here there be dragons." In *Sagittas* no demons lurk, save those that enter with us. In Royo's eternal eye there is only the sanctity of humanity—its roots, its future, and its meaning.

Royo says, "the painting is sufficient because its language is simple and its message direct." However, the effect is as complex as the mechanism of the universe, relying as it does on the ability of humans to understand the logic of infinity. It is only the dictionary presented by the artist's *Sagittas* series that allows the viewer to speak of previously indescribable relationships, and through newly discovered intertwining of the known and that which only an artist could first give thought, to rise above antiquated principles of gravity.

So, *Ritmo* bids the viewer welcome, and promises to guide one over new terrain—except, of course, these worlds have existed through time eternal, only we lacked the imaginative eyes of perception, and agile tongue with which to conjure realities existing within ancient metaphors.

Sagittas: in Latin, *Sagittas* is the arrow, and *Sagittario* is the archer. Taken together with the artist's presentation of the translation through visual poetry, the concept of *Sagittas* must be understood as one of perceptible motion rather than linguistic manipulation. It is the arc, described by the arrow freed from the archer's bow and traversing space, which may be seen as the key. However, merely tracing a missile's trajectory would be so simplistic as to present no invitation to further examination. Never in the *Sagittas* portraiture is an arrow seen to fly. Instead, the viewer is invited to explore, along with the artist, the mechanism and intention of the flight, and to attempt to glimpse the destined mark.

In image after image Royo presents his fellow sojourners with a bow—the propulsion that drives the arrow's flight. The bow, itself arc-shaped,

The arc is a flight of sparrows...
...The arc is the planetary path between horizons...

describes its intended purpose: to use an arc to create another arc. Just as life begets life, and growth insists on further development, the artist may have intuited one of the universal predicates.

The arc is a flight of sparrows, majestically soaring across a sky dappled with gentle azure and pink, or in bold defiance of heavens awake with the thunder of deep royal and navy and winds that drive clouds of ripple in an attempt to deprive the delicate birds of their destiny. The arc is the planetary path between horizons; it is the connection between what is perceptible and that which is theoretical; a visualization of the irresistible force.

The suggestion of an arc becomes, in Royo's deft hand, a paradigm of life: insistent and sustaining in spite of logic that predicts extinction. Yet, the actuality of the bow is a geometric perfection, the simile of logic. The combination of scientific principle and artistic expression is one intended by the artist, who has said that:

"Mathematics and painting have always been close — color complements, rather than contrasts— and geometry has always walked hand-in-hand with art. In all pictorial creation there is architectural depth. At the base of all architectural creations is a wide range of images and color. From this (contrast) radiates a tremendous force which communicates directly with our sensitivity."

It is precisely the artist's sensitivity that makes his new cycle both artistically and philosophically compelling. In the *Sagittas* works, spontaneous freedom of artistic styling is combined with geometric discipline, and expressed in classical imagery. The result is a post-Euclidean physics that provides a stepping stone to understanding the infinite. In this regard Royo fulfills his own destiny: the historian posits the question and the physicist

He has managed to suggest a world just beyond our sight.

demonstrates the responsive probabilities. It is, however, the great artist, who is sufficiently sensitive to the arc of life, the world, and its position —both temporal and infinite— in the mechanism of existence, who sees reality on the far side of the arc, and looses connecting arrows. It is the artist with the appeal of such universal vision, who suggests the road down which answers lie.

In demonstration of the hypothesis, it must be noted that Royo has chosen to portray his vision of *Sagittas* in classical expressions, using the very language of the ancient philosophers who provided the construct of modern —and post-modern— explorations. He presents a Grecian idyll of such linear and tonal harmonics that the wayfarer, is propelled, like the suggestive arrows from youth's bow in *La Cinta Dorada*, along an arc that hums of human destiny. The figures themselves peer into an unseen future as they sight along the arrow path. In a demonstration of the artist's use of arcs defining arcs, while viewing this work one finds oneself straining —actually arching ones neck— in an attempt to look over the youthful shoulders, and catch a glance, however fleeting, of that which those children see beyond their canvas confines. Could it be the future? Is that the reason Royo deliberately draws the viewer's attention beyond the corners of his picture? He has managed to suggest a world just beyond our sight, just as the arrow will fall to earth just beyond the apogee of the sightline.

Within the present, the ribbons flying behind the figure can be taken as a jetstream; a shadow of the arrows path from the present to the future. The artistic structure employed by the artist, is one that first causes one to explore the confines of the canvas, and then directs the vision beyond. Metaphorically, the use of this technique implies that there is existence beyond that of the picture. This suggestion, however, is not limited to a future beyond today. It speaks also of reality beyond the scope of human vision.

... greater awareness awaits discovery.

It is a truism that an artist is the present of his past, and his expression is the sum of his experience and background. When understood from this vantage, Royo's upbringing and education, both academic and religious, predicted the present direction of his work.

The creative process begins not with an idea, but with a subconscious synthesizing of various memories. As a photograph of recollection is developed, it is studied and compared against present understanding. The result is the ecstasy of discovery. What follows is the crafting of the artist's conclusions. What separates the truly fine artist from the artisan, is the innate ability of the former to construct on his canvas the thrill of his first understanding, and the prowess to do so with a deftness that allows the viewer to experience the moment of discovery.

If one is truly to attempt to share the Royo image, it is necessary to recall that, as a young man — probably of an age with the figures portrayed in the *Sagittas* canvases — the artist has received a classical education. Such an education presented by a family with a strong intellectual base, included classical thought, science, and mathematics. The day's most current understandings would have been carefully fed to the growing child, eventually to become the vocabulary through which he would find expression. This portion of the Royo resume is everywhere present in the *Sagittas* paintings. The works even present a jetstream of the modern response to Euclidean postulates; more than a single parallel line may be drawn through a point — the importance of the arc in Royo's architectural statement. In fact is the absolute logic of the Greek mathematician, but the result varies with the greater knowledge of the present. At the same time, suggested in that maturation of human understanding is the fact that greater awareness awaits discovery.

For mankind it must be sufficient that God is in the process.

The *Sagittas* cycle presents the artist's developing philosophy in the logical language of his past. But, logical progress alone cannot account for the emotion impact of the work comprising this series. For this one must seek explanation in the artist's religious training. It is the juxtapositioning of philosophical and scientific logic against the emotion of faith which creates most of the tension inherent in the present compositions. The children inhabiting these paintings might just be emblematic of seekers of a faith that is coexistent with all we continue to learn of the universe. Does *The Big Bang Theory* preclude the existence of God and the promise of life beyond this? The answer is not the artist's to give. Royo is engaged in the search for truth. The gaze of his creations promises a greater understanding beyond the fall of the land. The arc of the arrow path intimates that there is an interpolation of science and faith. In the expression of the artist's search is a statement learned at the Tower of Babel: it is not within the ability of humans to see God. We, at best, may glimpse God's presence in the ongoing operation of the universal mechanism, and from this know that God is the logical originator. For mankind it must be sufficient that God is in the process, and Royo, engaged in the creative process has come near to presenting a reassurance that all is not chaos: there is order in the universe.

Susan Lynn Solomon

First Edition 1998
Copyright© 1998 Editorial La Máscara
Copyright© 1998 Royo
Printed in Valencia, Spain.

Publisher
Editorial La Máscara, S.L.
Plaza Papa Juan Pablo II, 5-b
46015-Valencia, Spain.

Director: Enrique Calabuig Giménez
Cover Design: Lucía Mateu and Vicente Blanes
Layout: Esther Cidoncha
Texts: Alberto de la Hera and Susan Lynn Solomon
Photography: Juan García
Translation: Mireya Pí and Jennifer Bradburn
General Coordinator: María Angeles Pí
Proofreader: Celso Andrés Marqués
Art Producer: Margarita Llin
Production Manager: José Angel Pastor Giménez
U.S. Supervisors: Greg Bloch and Kevin Frest
Photomechanical Reproduction: Gamma 4, Valencia, Spain.
Printed by: Sorell Impresores S. A., Valencia, Spain.
Bookbinding and handling: Grafo, S. A. Bilbao, Spain.
PRINTING PAPER:
Fly Leaf: Fedrigoni Nettuno Blu Navy 300gr.
Text: Conqueror Contour 300gr.
Reproductions: Couché Ideal Premier Brillo 300gr.

All rights reserved by the Publisher under International and Pan-American Copy right Conventions. No part of this book may be reproduced or utilized in any form or by any means, electronic or mechanical, including photocopying, recording, or by any information storage and retrieval system, without permission in writing from the publisher. Sale of this book does not transfer by the copyright holder its exclusive right to prepare derivative works. The Ninth Circuit Court of appeals has ruled that removing individual prints or page prints from compilation books for sale to the public, without consent of copyright holders, comprises the making of derivative works and infringes the exclusive right of the copyright holders. Violators may be subject to civil and/or criminal penalties.

ISBN: 84-7974-413-8

e-mail: agora@agora.es
http://www.agora.es/royo.htm